Too nice

Published by
M A G I N A T I O N   P R E S S
An Educational Publishing Foundation Book
American Psychological Association
750 First Street, NE
Washington, DC 20002

For more information about our books, including a complete catalog,
please write to us, call 1-800-374-2721, or visit our website at
www.maginationpress.com.

Editor: Darcie Conner Johnston
Art Director: Susan K. White
The text type is Bookman
Printed by Phoenix Color, Rockaway, New Jersey

Library of Congress Cataloging-in-Publication Data

Pellegrino, Marjorie White.
Too nice / by Marjorie White Pellegrino ; illustrated by Bonnie Matthews.
p. cm.
Summary: While gardening with her grandfather after
a rough first week of fourth grade, Amy learns that it's sometimes better
to stand up for herself, rather than just trying to be nice.
ISBN 1-55798-917-6 (alk. paper) — ISBN 1-55798-918-4 (alk. paper)
[1. Self-esteem — Fiction. 2. Friendship — Fiction. 3. Schools — Fiction.
4. Grandfathers — Fiction. 5. Gardening — Fiction.]
I. Matthews, Bonnie J., 1963- ill. II. Title.

PZ7.P3637 To 2002
[Fic]—dc21   2002025490

Manufactured in the United States of America
10 9 8 7 6 5 4 3 2 1

Too Nice

written by
Marjorie White Pellegrino

illustrated by
Bonnie Matthews

MAGINATION PRESS • WASHINGTON, DC

Dear Reader,

Being nice is a good thing. The world works better when people are considerate toward each other. But you can be too nice, and that doesn't feel good.

Many kids are just like Amy in this book. Even I was just like Amy when I was her age. Kids sometimes think that if they don't do what other people ask, then others won't like them anymore or will get mad. But as Amy discovers (and as you have probably noticed in your own life), it just isn't possible to please everybody. It may even seem that the more you try, the more other people get annoyed at you or take advantage of you. And you end up feeling sad, angry, resentful, or just plain tired.

On the other hand, when you consider your own wants and needs too, or promises you've already made, or responsibilities you already have, something wonderful happens. You have more energy for other people. They respect you. They may be upset for a moment if they don't get what they want, but they still like you. In fact, they probably like you better, because you are someone they can trust to be honest and dependable. And that feels good all around.

If you're too nice like Amy, you don't have to keep being too nice. Notice the times when being nice feels bad. Does this happen when you are at school, or soccer practice, or your neighbor's house? Does it happen when you're with certain friends, or your big brother, or teammates, or the kids you babysit? Just like Amy, you can practice being "just right" nice. Think of times when you were too nice, and then practice being friendly yet sticking up for what you think is right or best. Practice in front of a mirror, or with a good friend or family member. When those situations come up again, you'll be more prepared to stick up for yourself. The more you do it, the easier it will get.

Sometimes I still end up being too nice. But now I know that I can say no. Or I can ask for more time to think about it. Or I can even change my mind and say, "I'm sorry, I didn't understand how much time this would take." I feel better, and so do the people around me. And so will you.

All the best,

MARJORIE WHITE PELLEGRINO

Contents

For Steve and Evan — MWP

For my sister, Linda Paul, who has always helped
in time of need — BM

CHAPTER 1

The Baseball

Fourth grade started off on the wrong foot.

"Here, Amy!" Micah yelled from across the playground. He bent his knees a little and slapped his hands together, then held them open like a catcher in a real baseball game. Amy looked at Micah with a big question mark on her face.

"Can we have the ball, Amy?" Micah asked, coming closer.

Amy didn't know what to do.

"Come on, Amy," Micah said, now standing next to her. He pointed at the field behind him. "We're ready to play, and you're just standing there. You're not using the ball."

Micah was right. She wasn't using it right that minute, and Amy didn't want Micah to be mad at her. She handed the ball over. Micah threw the ball up high and then ran to catch it with a *thwap*.

"Thanks," he called back. Then he tossed the ball on ahead to his friends in the field.

"Where's the ball?" Kate asked as she ran up to Amy. Amy pointed over at Micah.

Kate frowned. "Why does he have it?

I thought you took it from the bin!"
    Amy shrugged. "I did, but...,"
Amy's voice trailed off. She didn't
know what to say.

"Great, Amy. Now we don't have a ball for our game," said Kate. She turned and ran off to join a group of girls playing jump rope.

"But I was just trying to be nice," Amy thought as she walked back toward the school, kicking up pebbles as she went.

CHAPTER 2

The Cookies

At lunch the next day, Amy offered Kate some of the lettuce she and her grandfather had grown in their garden. "It's the best!" Amy said. Kate agreed that it wasn't bad for a vegetable.

"Skip the lettuce," Marisa said and pointed to Amy's bag of chocolate chip cookies. "But those cookies look *reeeally* good."

Amy offered the bag to Marisa. "Help yourself."

"Can I have one, too?" Micah asked from farther down the table. By the time the bag got back to Amy, the cookies were all gone. When no

one was looking, Amy licked her
finger like a postage stamp and
pressed it inside the bottom of the
bag to pick up every crumb. The
crumbs did taste *reeeally* good, but
that made her feel really bad. Her
mouth watered for a whole cookie,
and all she could do was hope that
there would be some left at home for
an after-school snack.

CHAPTER 3

On The Bus

On the bus the next afternoon, Hannah said, "I want the front seat. *Pleeeease*, Amy? May I have this seat?"

Oh no, it was going to happen again.

Amy didn't know what to say. She didn't want to hurt Hannah's feelings, and she was afraid Hannah wouldn't

like her if she said no like she wanted
to. So she scooted over to make room,
even though she was supposed to be
saving the seat for Kate. Kate always
sat with Amy on the bus ride home.
They had been sitting together ever
since the first day of kindergarten.

Kate stood in line right behind
Hannah. She tilted her head and
looked back and forth from Hannah
to Amy. She didn't look happy.
Actually, she looked angry at Amy.

"Thanks," Hannah said at Amy's
offer to move over and make room,

"but Matthew is going to sit with me.
Could you move, please?"

Amy still didn't know what to say.
Well, that wasn't really true. She
wanted to say, "No, I don't want to
move," but she couldn't get the words

out. So she just gathered her books
and lunch box and found another seat
farther back. Kate passed right by
Amy like Amy was invisible.

On the ride home, Amy sat by
herself watching the houses and trees

pass by. In the window she could also see the reflection of the kids on the bus. Happy kids. Amy felt like she didn't belong in the reflection. She wasn't feeling very happy. In fact, she felt rotten. As rotten as she could imagine. As rotten as a moldy peach at the bottom of a fruit bin.

When Kate passed Amy's seat on her way off the bus, she said, "You're too nice." Then Amy found out that she could feel even worse than rotten.

CHAPTER 4

Lunch Table Duty

On Friday morning, Amy read the list of jobs on the board. Kate and Marisa had lunch table duty. Maybe this was her chance to work things out with Kate.

"Hey! Need help cleaning the tables?" Amy asked Kate and Marisa when she was finished eating. "Thanks, Amy!" they said together.

Kate put her sponge in Amy's left hand and Marisa flipped hers onto Amy's right. They turned and headed out the door to the playground.

Amy opened her mouth, but not one word came out. She felt her eyebrows reach skyward and her face turn hot. This wasn't what Amy had in mind at all. She thought she was offering to help so that they could all

go outside together and have more time to play. Instead, she was stuck with the whole job.

She wiped the messy tables all by herself, with both sponges. Angrily, she swept up bits of sandwiches, cookie crumbs, and broken chips. While she worked, her mouth was a hard, straight line, and she thought about what games she could be

playing if she was outside with everyone else. But as soon as she finished the last table, the bell rang. Recess was over, and Amy didn't get outside for a single minute.

By the end of the first week of fourth grade, Amy felt tired. She was tired of feeling sad and mad. She was tired of sharing her food, tired of moving for other people, tired of giving things away, and tired of being mostly alone. Amy was glad that today was Friday.

DING DING

CHAPTER 5

Too Nice?

Amy slept late on Saturday.
When she woke up and looked out her
window, she saw Grandpa at work in
the garden. She finished her breakfast
apple just as she reached the fence
and threw the core as far as she could
toward the woods for the rabbits.
Then she unlatched the gate and
entered the cool green garden.

"Morning," she said without the "good" to go with it. She crouched down and started pulling weeds.

"Good morning," said Grandpa cheerfully. "How are you today?" Amy shrugged but didn't answer.

"Cat got your tongue?" Grandpa wondered aloud after a few minutes.

Amy was quiet a little bit longer. Then she told him. She told him about Micah and the ball. She told him about not getting to eat her cookies. She told him about losing her seat on the bus. "The last straw was yesterday," said Amy. "I offered to help, and I ended up getting stuck doing the lunch tables all by myself."

"You know, you can be too nice," Grandpa said, pulling a clump of grass from the edge of the garden. He shook off the dirt and threw it into the bucket for the compost pile.

Amy was glad that Grandpa was looking at the weeds he was pulling and not at her. She didn't want him to see that smunched-up, almost-ready-to-cry look on her face.

Amy tore off a leaf of lettuce and chewed on it. Kate had called her "too

27

nice" too. Amy drew a big breath into
her lungs and let it out all at once like
air from a balloon. She felt confused.
She just didn't get it. What did it
mean to be "too nice," and why did it
feel so bad? And why did she keep
doing it?

"You taught me not to be rude,"
Amy said after a few minutes, her pile
of weeds growing.

"You can stand up for yourself

without being rude," Grandpa said.

"But if I do, the other kids won't like me," Amy said. "Or they might get mad at me."

"I'm not so sure about that," Grandpa replied with a smile. He nodded his head toward the street. Kate was walking up to the garden.

CHAPTER 6

Friends Again

Kate arrived just as Amy and Grandpa were weeding the last row. "Need some help?" she offered.

"Perfect timing," Grandpa said. "I promised Grandma I'd tag along for the grocery shopping. Looks like she's about ready to go." Grandpa got up slowly and headed for the garage.

Amy and Kate talked while they worked. By the time the last of the weeds were pulled, Amy felt like the bus and the lunchroom sadness had melted away like snow in the sun.

Suddenly Kate threw a clump of weeds at Amy's feet. Bits of dirt sprayed her legs.

"Eeew!" Amy squealed with a grin. She pretended to give a wind-up pitch and then let her clump of weeds hit just shy of Kate's feet. "You're it!" Amy laughed and ran out of the garden. She forgot all about the gate.

no More Lettuce

Kate had gone home and Amy was helping Mom clean up the kitchen when they heard Grandma and Grandpa's car pull into the driveway. When Amy went to the back door, she saw the car doors open but no Grandma and Grandpa.

"Hey, the car's there, but they're not!" Amy said to Mom.

"Where'd they go?" Mom
wondered, peeking out the window.

"I'll go see," Amy said.

She went outside and around the
corner of the house. Grandma and
Grandpa were shooing a rabbit out of
the garden.

"Get going, you bandit," Grandma
was saying. "This is not your dinner."

Amy's throat tightened. She felt like she had just swallowed a peach pit and it was stuck halfway down.

"Sure looks like the lettuce is done for the season," Grandpa said, pointing at the row of little green nubs chewed to the ground. "That rabbit has the same favorite that you do, Amy. Didn't bother much else except for the lettuce."

"It's my fault," Amy said, all of her good feelings gone like a popped bubble. "I forgot about the gate."

"My lettuce queen, I bet that's one mistake you won't make again," Grandpa said, patting her shoulder. "It's okay. Making mistakes is part of how we learn things."

"You'll probably miss that lettuce more than anyone else will, anyway," Grandma said.

After dinner, as the late summer sun was starting to set, Grandpa and

Amy carried some leftover scraps from the kitchen outside. Amy felt a wave of misery wash over her as they passed the garden.

"I'd imagine that rabbit loves it when we give it scraps," Grandpa said, like he was reading her mind. "But when we have to scare it out of the garden, it's probably not too happy."

They scraped the plate into a

rabbit-sized pile at the edge of the yard.

"It's better for me and for the rabbit if I keep my fence up. Otherwise, I'd have a garden of nothing, and that rabbit would have a case of the jitters from being scared off all the time."

Amy took Grandpa's hand as they walked back to the house.

"Same thing with people," Grandpa continued. "If you want to bring extra cookies to share, that's a fine thing. But make sure you hold on to what you'd like to eat before you pass the bag around."

Grandpa turned to face Amy when they reached the back porch. "Think of it this way, Amy. You can put a fence around yourself just like the one I put around our garden. Not a real fence, of course. But learning to say no when you don't want to give something up is like building an imaginary fence. It's a way of protecting yourself, just like I protect the garden. Maybe if you stand up for yourself you'll feel happier."

"But I don't know how to put a fence around me. How can I say no without making someone mad or hurting their feelings?" Amy asked.

"Remember, when there's a fence

around the garden, the rabbit is
happier, too," Grandpa smiled. "People
usually like us better when we stand
up for ourselves, even though it seems
like they wouldn't. And if they do get
mad at you, it will probably be for just

a few minutes and then it will pass."

Amy wasn't so sure about that. She always thought that if people got angry at you they wouldn't like you anymore. But she was ready to try Grandpa's idea. She didn't want the second week of fourth grade to be anything like the first week.

So Grandpa and Amy practiced.

CHAPTER 8

Good Fences

First Amy pretended she was Micah, while Grandpa played the role of Too Nice Amy.

"Here!" Amy shouted in a Micah voice, and she crouched down and put out her hands like a catcher.

"Oh, here Micah, take the ball. Anything else you need, you just ask and I'll run and get it for you!" Grandpa

after I'm finished

said in his Too Nice Amy voice.

"You're making fun of me!" Amy laughed.

"Oh, I'm very sorry. I didn't mean to make you think I was making fun of you," said Grandpa in Amy's soft voice.

"Let's try it again, only this time I'll be the Good Fence Amy," Grandpa said.

Amy nodded. "Here!" she yelled in her Micah-like voice. Instead of throwing the pretend ball, Grandpa said kindly but firmly, "Do you want to play with us, Micah? Because if you do, that would be great. If you don't, we'll give you the ball when we're done with our game."

As Amy practiced, the words came out easier than she thought they would. Maybe this wouldn't be so hard.

CHAPTER 9

Just Right Amy

On Monday morning, Amy boarded the school bus and sat in the front seat. At the next stop, Hannah got on.

"Would you move?" Hannah asked, standing in the aisle. *"Pleeease?"*

"There's an empty seat right behind me," Amy answered firmly with a smile. "Why don't you sit there?"

Hannah didn't budge. "I want the front seat, Amy. Please let me have it." Other kids piled up behind Hannah, but she just stood there looking at Amy with puppy-dog eyes. Amy felt like doing what Hannah wanted, but she remembered what Grandpa told her. She didn't have to give up her seat.

"Stop holding up the works," the bus driver told Hannah. Hannah groaned and sat down in the seat

behind Amy. At the next stop, Kate and Matthew got on. Kate sat with Amy, and Matthew sat in the next seat with Hannah. The four of them were laughing together, all friends, by the time the bus rolled to a stop in front of the school.

After lunch, Amy and Kate drew a yellow road and a green castle on the playground pavement with colored chalk. Amy told Kate about how she was learning to build imaginary fences and trying to stop being Too Nice Amy.

Halfway through recess, Micah came over.

"Can I use some of those colors?" he asked.

Amy reached for the box.

Kate stopped drawing and looked at Amy. Their eyes met for just a moment.

Amy put the box back down.

"We're not done yet, Micah," she said. "You can be next in line to use the chalk, unless you want to work with us. We're making the Emerald City from *The Wizard of Oz*. You could help."

"Cool," Micah said.

He turned out to be quite an artist.

And Amy thought fourth grade might turn out to be pretty good after all.

About the Author

MARJORIE WHITE PELLEGRINO studied psychology and worked as a trainer before she began writing professionally. "I discovered that real people, not just magical ones, could be writers," she says. In addition to many magazine and newspaper articles, she is the author of *My Grandma's the Mayor* and *I Don't Have an Uncle Phil Anymore*, both published by Magination Press.

Ms. Pellegrino shares her passion for the written word by teaching creative writing, journaling, book making and poetry to all ages through schools, libraries, social service agencies, and community organizations.

She grew up in New York State and now lives in Tucson, Arizona, with her husband and son and the desert dwellers that visit their yard.

About the Illustrator

BONNIE MATTHEWS taught herself illustration while she was a student of graphic design at Virginia Commonwealth University. In addition to the many children's books she has illustrated, her whimsical people and animals have appeared in more than 100 magazines worldwide, and on gift wrap, greeting cards, tin cans, and even the cover of the *Land's End Kids* catalog.

Ms. Matthews donates part of her efforts to concerns and organizations she cares about, such as the Baltimore Zoo, the Wilderness Society, and Johns Hopkins Children's Center. She lives in Baltimore and is a frequent speaker at local schools, where she encourages children to draw and follow their creative aspirations. "I have a special interest in children's books," she says, "because I think that pictures help promote reading, and I personally had a difficult time learning to read."